Andy finds a Turtle

By Nan Holcomb

Illustrated By Dot Yoder

JASON & NORDIC PUBLISHERS
HOLLIDAYSBURG, PENNSYLVANIA

Books in this series:

ANDY FINDS A TURTLE
DANNY AND THE MERRY-GO-ROUND
HOW ABOUT A HUG

Text Copyright © 1987 Jason and Nordic Publishers
Illustrations copyright © 1088 Dorothy Yoder

Library of Congress Cataloging-in-Publication Data
Holcomb, Nan, date.
    Andy finds a turtle.

    Summary: Andy's physical therapist calls him a turtle one day when he is feeling uncooperative, and thus begins a search to find a turtle, during which he becomes a small hero and learns something important about himself.

    [1. Physically handicapped — Fiction. 2. Turtles — Fiction.]
I. Yoder, Dot, ill.   II Title.
PZ7.H6972An   1988   [E]   87-29771

ISBN 0-944727-13-1

Printed in the U.S.A.

for Jason

Every Monday Andy had physical therapy — PT for short — because his arms and legs didn't work as arms and legs should.

One Monday morning Andy's PT teacher tried very hard to make Andy's arms and legs move, but Andy didn't feel like helping. His arms curled tight to his chest and his legs felt very comfortable pulled up tight. Miss Jones tugged and tugged, but they wouldn't move.

Finally she said, in a very cross voice, "You're not a boy this morning. You're a turtle."

Andy scowled at Miss Jones, but inside he said, "What's a turtle?" Miss Jones didn't think much of turtles. Andy could tell by the way she said it.

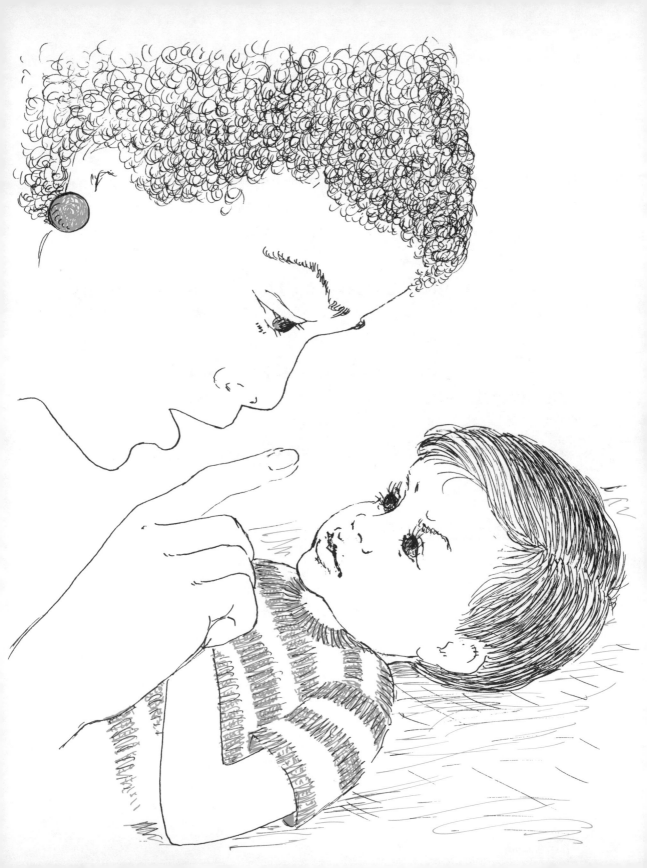

But what *is* a turtle?

Andy listened closely to TV.

He listened closely to the stories Mommy read.

He listened closely when people talked. And he wondered.

Are turtles big and scary? Are turtles small and slimy?

Nobody mentioned turtles.

One day Andy's big cousin came for a visit. Dan liked to help Andy get ready for the day. He pretended Andy was an airplane and flew him out of bed and around the room.

He changed Andy's shirt and picked up his back brace. "Let's get you into your turtle shell," Dan said.

Andy opened his eyes wide. My turtle shell, he thought, as the back brace slipped around his chest. Am I a turtle? A turtle has arms and legs that make Miss Jones cross. And, a turtle has a shell. Are they big legs and little shells? Oh, my. I have another problem. What's a shell?

A shell. Maybe if I find a shell — that may help me find a turtle.

Andy listened closely to TV.

He listened closely to people talking.

One day he heard the word in his own kitchen where Mommy was baking a cake and Daddy was drying dishes.

"Whoops!" Mommy said as she dropped something. "Would you pick up that shell for me, dear?"

After lunch Andy watched the baby while Mommy and Daddy cleaned up the mess. As he lay on the blanket beside Sue, a strange looking stone moved onto the blanket, straight toward Sue's face. As it moved closer, Andy saw two little eyes and a mouth. Would it bite Sue? he wondered. He wanted to call, "Mommy! Daddy!" and get help. He had to move or yell or do something.

He tried hard to move his arm, harder than he'd ever tried for Miss Jones. Finally, his hand moved and gave the rock a good hard bump. The head disappeared and Andy let out a yell.

Mommy and Daddy came running. Andy stared at the rock. Would it move again, or had he imagined it had moved before? The head poked slowly out and darted back.

Andy looked at Mommy. "Were you afraid?" she asked. Andy nodded his head and blinked his eyes very fast to say 'yes!'

"I think he kept it from getting on Sue," Daddy said. Andy blinked, 'yes' even faster. He wanted to say, what is it?

"Do you know what this is?" Daddy asked as he picked up the rock. Andy stared. He didn't.

"It's a turtle" Daddy said. "See it has legs inside. When he's frightened or not feeling like company, he pulls in his head and legs and not a thing anyone can do will get him to move."

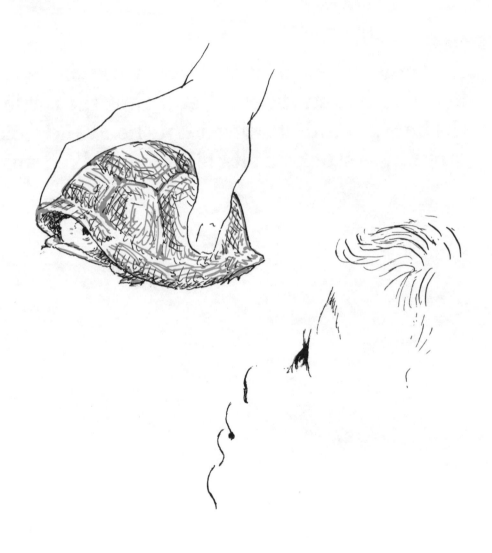

Andy looked closely. There were the legs all folded tight and useless. Daddy put the turtle on the bare ground. It stuck out its head and looked around. It stuck out its legs and walked away.

So that's a turtle, Andy thought. Hmm-m-m. I guess I am a turtle sometimes, he chuckled to himself. I have a shell and sometimes not a thing Miss Jones does will get me to move. Andy stretched his arm out as far as he could stretch it and waved 'good-by' to the turtle.

A turtle is very handsome . . . for a turtle. Andy smiled. But, I'm very glad I'm not really a turtle. I guess from now on I'd rather be a boy every day . . . even on Mondays!

And he was!